Attila the Bluebottle
and More Wild Stories

'There are times when life is perfect.
For Attila the bluebottle it was one of
those times. When he actually
thought about it, every single day of
his life had been perfect and he had
been alive for a whole week. He had
spent the morning inside a fish head
at the bottom of the dustbin and was
so full up he could hardly move.
Everywhere he looked it was the
same view of paradise. Fat lazy
bluebottles full of rotten fish
staggered around with big contented
grins on their faces.'

Twelve wild stories from a garden.

Attila the Bluebottle and More Wild Stories

Colin Thompson

Illustrations by the author

Hodder
Children's
Books

a division of Hodder Headline plc

Typeset by Hewer Text Composition Services, Edinburgh

Printed and bound in Great Britain by Cox & Wyman Ltd,
Reading, Berks.

Hodder Children's Books
A Division of Hodder Headline plc
338 Euston Road
London NW1 3BH

Contents

This book is dedicated
to the memory of
Wallace,
1978–1990,
who sleeps in the garden.

Waking Up

At the end of a quiet street at the edge of a large town, between tidy houses and tidy gardens, was a wild place. Once it had been a garden like those on either side, with a neat lawn and straight rows of flowers, but some years before, the old lady who had lived there had moved away and since then the garden had become a dark and mysterious jungle. In the middle of this wild place was an empty house, called fourteen, that was slowly disappearing behind crawling bushes and overgrown trees.

As time passed the grass grew taller, burying the path from the front gate, the ivy crawled up the walls and slipped in through the broken windows. The trees wove new branches together and the garden became a closed and secret place.

In the jungle the honeysuckle filled the air with heavy dreams, and animals that had nowhere else to go made their homes in its welcoming branches and secret places. Moles and rats that had been driven from the tidy gardens all around took refuge there. Beyond the edge of the abandoned lawn, under a thick bramble bush, a chicken lived in an orange box, and up on the roof of the house crows had filled the chimneys with years of nests. Rabbits that could never find enough to eat anywhere else lived in a wild warren at the bottom of the garden beneath a crowded hedge. Beyond the hedge, through brambles and giant hogweed taller than men, a dusty towpath ran beside an old canal and across the canal was a desperate place of crumbling factories and fractured concrete.

The years passed and then one day as spring began to push the winter aside the old lady's nephew lifted away the broken gate and took his family to live in the neglected house.

Windows stiff with age were forced open and given new panes of glass and a coat of paint. The branches that had grown across them were

chopped down and sunshine crept into the house for the first time in years. As the rooms grew warm again the dampness that had reached up to the highest ceilings was driven back into the earth.

In three quick weeks, the cobwebs were swept away, the holes that had let the rats in were filled up and the crows' nests were pushed out of the chimneys with stiff brushes.

When the chimneys were clear they lit fires in every room. The chopped-down branches crackled as the flames ate through them and filled the air with sweet smelling smoke. The thin shoots of plants that had crept into the house behind the plaster shrivelled away and in a few days it was as if they had never been there. Once again the house was back in human hands.

Out in the garden the air was filled with nervous talk as the animals sat and waited. The homeless crows huddled in the tall trees and made everyone else miserable. Eventually they made new nests in the high branches, but for months afterwards they complained to anyone who would listen.

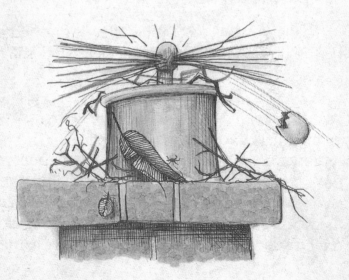

'Just wait,' they said. 'When they've finished with the house, they'll come out here and kill the garden.'

The other animals said nothing because they were all frightened that what the crows were saying might be true.

'Of course, they'll wait until we've built new nests,' said the crows. 'They'll wait till we're all nicely settled in with fresh eggs ready to hatch, then they'll come out and chop everything down until it's as flat and dead as all the other gardens.'

It looked as though the crows were right, for as spring turned into early summer the man bought a bright red lawnmower and attacked the back garden. The machine flew over the grass like an eagle, tearing it to pieces as it passed. The green tunnels that the mice had made over the years vanished in a minute, leaving a wide open yellow space that was unsafe to cross. From her box under the bush, Ethel the chicken sat very still and watched him go by. From the tops of the trees the crows looked down, too scared of the man to go and pick up the worms he had disturbed. All the terrible things they had predicted were coming true.

7

Every weekend the family pulled out the weeds that had grown around the house and swept up the dead leaves. They cut back the ivy until it was no taller than a dog and piled everything up into a huge bonfire in the old vegetable garden.

In the evenings as the days grew longer the man sat in an armchair by the French windows, gazed out across the tidy lawn at the dense undergrowth beyond and fell asleep. Sometimes he would wake up just as the light was fading away and see the rabbits and hedgehogs moving softly in the shadows. Sometimes he would see the blackbirds hopping across the grass and other birds flying in from all around to roost in the tall trees. Maybe something told him that if he cut everything down they would all go away, or maybe he was just lazy, but as the summer grew warmer his enthusiasm for gardening grew less and less.

The animals grew more and more restless. They knew the people would chop everything down. That's what people did, they only had to look at every other garden to see that. But the family finished playing with their bonfire and then left everything alone. Some of the smaller, more nervous animals like the voles and the shrews moved out into the narrow strip of wasteland by the canal, but for most of them there was nowhere else to go and they just had to watch and wait.

'They're just biding their time,' said the crows.

'What for?' asked Ethel the chicken, but no one knew.

And then something happened that made the family make up its mind once and for all.

In the next house there were two miserable people who complained all day long. As she complained about the sunshine, he complained about the cold. When he complained about the noise, she said it was too quiet. They complained to each other about everything and when they could no longer stand to listen to their own voices, they wrote and complained to the newspapers. They hated everything and everyone but most of all they hated the overgrown garden next door that dropped leaves onto their tidy lawn and cut out the daylight and threatened them with its untamed life.

'My wife wants you to cut down the trees by our fence,' said the nervous man. He stood shuffling from foot to foot on the doorstep while his wife hid behind her plastic curtains.

'Why?' said the man.

'She says they drop leaves on her flowerbeds,' said the nervous man.

'That's alright,' said the woman. 'You can keep them, we've got loads more.' In the next room their two children laughed and the miserable man went away. His miserable wife came to the door and she complained about the squirrels and the hedgehogs and the rabbits and the mice.

'I didn't even know we had squirrels,' said the man. The miserable woman went away and wrote a letter to the town hall who lost it in a wastepaper basket with the eighty-six others she had sent them. Seven times they went back to fourteen to complain and the last time they said they'd get the police. The family laughed and thanked them for saving them so much work, because whatever they had been planning to do in the garden they certainly weren't going to now.

'Anyone can have a rotary clothes drier in their garden,' said the woman after the miserable couple had gone back to their net curtains and pampered cat, 'but only special people get squirrels and hedgehogs.'

And they built a bird table and put out nesting boxes for the bluetits.

The family's two children tunnelled down the garden, crawling like voles through the undergrowth and above a clearing of soft grass in the branches of a wide oak tree they built a tree house. They lay flat on their stomachs and looked down into the overgrown pond as the moorhens led their chicks away through the ferns to the canal.

When the lawn was green again the children played football. Round and round they ran, throwing a big blue ball in the air. A big blue ball which bounced and rolled and rolled and rolled right up to Ethel the chicken's box.

'Look, look, look,' shouted the little girl to her brother. They reached out and tickled Ethel in exactly the right place. The old chicken shut her eyes and felt all the loneliness of the past quiet years slip away.

The little girl tucked Ethel under her arm and carried her up to the house. The little boy ran beside her, smiling and laughing.

Later on, the man gave Ethel a smart new box with a label on the side that said 'BEST APPLES'. 'I am not a best apple,' said Ethel to herself as she settled down into her wonderful new straw. 'I am a chicken.'

'And I shall call you Doris,' said the little girl as she poured her out a mug of corn.

Nearly Spring

Long nights as black as sleep,
Short days bleached grey with cold,
The sun hangs weak as water
In a sky grown flat and old.

In oak trees stripped and brittle,
Round shouldered sparrows sleep.
Through grasses bent and broken,
Cold slow creatures creep.

As every night grows shorter
The air turns soft and warm.
Nature cracks her frozen teeth,
Spits frost across the lawn.

Long days as soft as smiles,
Short nights that rest the soul,
The moon hangs pale as violets
In a sky of speckled coal.

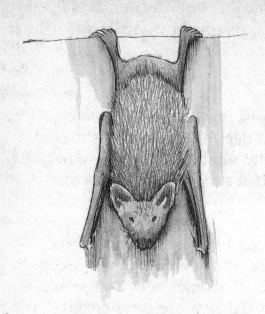

Albert the Bat

In the dark loft at the top of the house, in the darkest corner where the slates met the wall, lived a family of bats. They had lived there for as long as anyone could remember. Long before the old lady had left the house and even before she had been born, there had been bats under the roof. They were there even when Queen Victoria had been on the throne. They were an old and noble family treated with great respect by all the other animals apart from the moths who had been their supper for over a hundred years.

At one time there had been bats in every attic down the street, but now they had all gone except for this one family. One by one they had been driven out by loft conversions or killed by woodworm spray. Only under this roof, untouched and quiet like the garden below, was there any safety.

The last few winters had been long and cold. With no fires in the empty house, the air in the loft was cold and damp and the bats had hibernated right up to the end of spring. Now there were people in the house and warmth rising from the rooms below soaked through the chimneys next to the bats' roost. It was March outside but under the roof it felt like the beginning of summer. One by one the sleeping bats woke up. The crumbling plaster between the rafters was full of drowsy butterflies who had also woken up too early and the bats lived on them until the evenings grew warm enough to go outside.

The young bats, who had never hibernated before, woke up feeling very strange and unable to understand how they had got so much older in their sleep. They fluttered around in confusion, falling on to the tops of the ceilings and crawling around in the dust. Their mothers swooped and dived above them, coaxing them back into the air.

'If you stay like that with your feet on the ground,' they said, 'the blood will rush to your feet and you'll get dizzy.'

Of all the bats in the attic the oldest was Albert. He was twenty three years old and he was having trouble with his radar.

'I keep hearing voices in my head,' he said, 'far away voices that sound like men.'

'What are they saying?' asked the others.

'I don't know,' said Albert. 'It's too far away to tell.'

'Perhaps it's voices from the other side,' said Flossie, who believed in that sort of thing.

'The other side of what?' asked a young bat called Ryan.

'You know,' said Flossie, going all mysterious, 'voices from beyond.'

'Beyond what?' asked Ryan, trying to keep a straight face which can be difficult for a bat.

'Ryan,' called his mother, 'stop being cheeky to your Auntie Flossie.'

'I don't care where they're coming from,' said Albert. 'I want them to stop.'

'You're probably tired,' said Ryan's mother. 'You probably just need a rest.'

'A rest, a rest?' said Albert. 'We've been hibernating all winter, how could I need a rest?'

The trouble was that the voices in his head were interfering with his radar and it's radar that bats use to find their food. Every time Albert flew out into the garden to catch moths all he could hear was blurred noises like a ventriloquist's dummy shut in a suitcase.

The voices weren't always there. As the night moved on they grew less and less and in the early hours before dawn they usually went away all together. By then of course the other bats had caught the biggest moths and Albert had to make do with the stragglers that were still throwing themselves at the street light outside the house. They flung themselves at the brightly-lit glass and as they fell unconscious to the ground Albert swooped and caught them before the old cat waiting at the bottom of the lamppost could get them.

'I'm fed up always getting my food broken,' he said. 'They crash into the light and get all dented.'

'It could be worse,' said Ryan's mother. 'You could be a vampire bat and have to suck blood out of people's necks.'

'Or cow's bu . . ,' Ryan started to say, but his mother stopped him.

The nights grew shorter and warmer and the voices in Albert's head grew louder. He still couldn't make out what they were saying, but they were definitely getting stronger. All the other male bats had gone off to spend the summer in hollow trees and the deserted factories across the canal. The canal itself was a wonderful place for food. At dusk it was alive with insects that drove men away and drew bats in.

The loft was full of new born babies now and everyone was too busy looking after them to bother with Albert's problems. Twice a night all the mothers flew off to feed, leaving him alone with hundreds of tiny twittering creatures. He couldn't decide which was worse, the noise they made or the noise in his head.

And then one night one of the voices grew so loud that he understood what it was saying.

'Are you there?' it said. It was a man and he sounded in a bad mood.

'Err, yes, I'm here,' said Albert nervously.

'You'll have to speak louder than that,' said Flossie. 'They'll never hear you on the other side.' And they hadn't, for a few seconds later they called again.

'Oi mate, are you there?' it said.

'Oi mate?' said Albert. 'They're not very cultured, these spirits of yours, are they?'

'Answer it, quickly,' said Flossie, 'and shout this

time.'

'HELLO?' shouted Albert, but they still couldn't hear him, because a few seconds later the voice called out again and filled Albert's head up with a lot of very rude words, most of which he had never heard before. He repeated them to Flossie who looked shocked and then said in a low whisper: 'I think they must be from down there.'

'Down where?' said Ryan.

'Down there,' repeated Flossie. 'You know, H-E-L-L.'

'Ooerr,' said Ryan.

Albert thought that all this talk about spirits and ghosts was a load of rubbish but he went very quiet and put his wings over his head. He tried to sleep but the voices wouldn't go away. All night they shouted at him and all night he ignored them. And then, just before dawn, the man stopped calling him and a woman's voice came into his head and she spoke to him by name.

'Bert,' she said, 'can you go to the Golf Club?'

'They want me to go to the Golf Club,' he said to Flossie.

'Well then, we'd better go, hadn't we,' Flossie replied and together they flew off into the sunrise. As they coasted over the tall trees and out of the garden the voice said: 'You'd better fly, you should've been there hours ago.'

'Well, we're hardly going to walk, are we?' said Albert.

When they reached the Golf Club, the two bats slipped up under the eaves of the clubhouse and slept. That night when they woke up Albert could hear nothing but wonderful clear silence and the soft noises of moths fluttering in the dark. Nor did he ever hear the voices in his head again except on Saturday nights when the radio taxis came to collect the golfers at closing time.

Four Bluetits

Two bluetits were sitting on a branch looking across the garden at a wooden nesting box nailed to the back of the house. Two other bluetits were hopping in and out of the box.

'Look at it,' said Max. 'I ask you. Modern homes.'

'I know,' agreed Jim. 'Plywood rubbish.'

'I mean, that's not a home, not a proper home you'd want to bring kids into, is it?' said Max. 'I mean, where are the nice knot holes and the rough bark crawling with all those tasty insects? Where are the body lice hiding in the cracks?'

'Yeah, it's just a bloomin' box,' said Jim.

'I tell you what,' Max continued. 'You put a load of grass and fluff in there, six eggs and the wife, and the bottom'll fall out of it. You'll see.'

'I know,' agreed Jim, 'but you can't tell them, can you?'

'Tell them, tell them? I should think not. I've not had a minute's peace since those boxes were put up.'

'The man's put a couple of big ones up over there, see?' said Jim. 'And a pair of starlings were straight in there before he'd even put his hammer away.'

'Well, what do you expect with starlings,' laughed Max. 'Thick as two short planks.'

The two birds laughed so much they almost fell off their twig. Max hung upside down and said; 'Here, how many starlings does it take to change a lightbulb?'

'Dunno'

'None, because they're all too thick.'

The two birds began laughing so much that this time they did fall out of the tree.

'Well, you won't get me into one of them,' said Jim as they flew over to a new bird feeder. 'Not in a million years.'

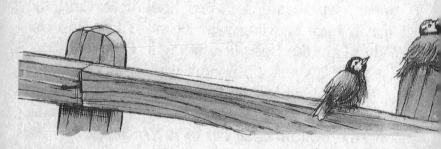

'Isn't it wonderful?' said Trixie, hopping out of the nesting box. 'A home of our own.'

'Gorgeous,' said Katie.

'Every modern convenience you could wish for,' said Trixie. 'Just look at that entrance hole, a perfect circle.'

'I envy you, I really do,' agreed Katie.

'And would you look at that perch. Go on, have a hop on it.'

'Ooh, isn't it fabulous,' said Katie, 'just the right size for your feet.'

'I know. And look at that lovely bit of felt on the top and those shiny little nails. That's quality, that is.'

'And what about Jim?' asked Katie. 'What does he think?'

'Think, think? He doesn't think,' said Trixie. 'He's too busy hanging round that new bird feeder all day showing off to the sparrows to think.'

'My Max won't have one,' said Katie. 'He says they'll fall to bits.'

'They'll outlast the pair of them,' laughed Trixie. 'My Jim's so fat from eating peanuts I shouldn't think he could even get in the door.'

'My old man's the same.'

'So fat they'll have to live in that big box over there,' laughed Trixie.

'Yeah, next to the stupid starlings,' roared Katie and they both shook so much with laughter that the nesting box fell off its hook onto the lawn.

'See,' said Max, looking down at the pieces of broken wood on the grass, 'I told you they weren't safe.'

DorisEthel

DorisEthel sat in her apple box looking across the lawn at the house. The sun was warm on her feathers, the air was soft and still and the old chicken soon fell asleep. As she slept she dreamt of days gone by when she had been young and there had been other chickens in the garden.

They had all lived in a smart hut with three nesting boxes and the garden had been full of fresh earth to scrape about in. In her dream there were worms as fat as carrots and there were fluffy yellow chicks round her feet looking up at her with love and admiration. And she dreamed of Eric. What a wonderful cockerel he had been, so tall and bossy and with such lovely tail feathers. DorisEthel could still remember how proud she

had felt every morning
when he had flown
onto the shed roof and
crowed his head off.
She could remember
too, running away just
before next door's
upstairs window
opened and the
bucketful of water
came flying out. Eric
may have been big and
beautiful but he had
also been very, very
stupid. Every
morning, just after his
third cock-a-doodle-
doo, he had been
soaked to the skin.
The window opened,
Eric looked up at the
noise and got the water
right in his face.

'I'm going down the
bottom of the garden
tomorrow,' he used to
say, but he always
forgot and DorisEthel
didn't see why she
should remind him.

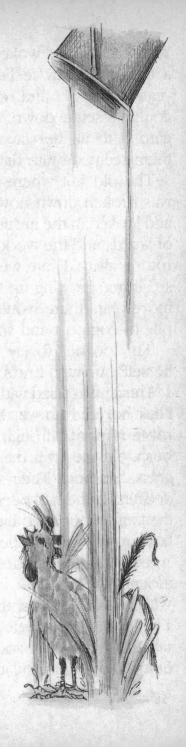

When DorisEthel woke up she was broody. It was a terrible fidgety feeling that she hadn't felt for years and years and no matter what she did she couldn't settle down. She wandered round the garden to all her favourite places, but none of them seemed quite right.

The old hut where all the chickens had lived was broken down now. She hopped up inside it and looked in the nesting boxes. They were all full of weeds and the wooden sides were broken and rotting away. There were holes in the roof and a small tree growing up through the floor. In a few more years there would be nothing left except a pile of compost and some rusty nails.

'I'm too old to lay an egg now,' she said to herself. 'Anyway, Eric's not here any more.'

The air was filled with the hum of early summer. Flies hovered above the bright grass and a lazy robin hopped through the branches of a nearby bush. On the lawn the children were lying in the grass, reading. Their mother was asleep in a deckchair. She had been knitting a cardigan but as the sun had climbed higher in the sky and the day had grown warmer she had nodded off.

'I wonder if she's dreaming of eggs,' DorisEthel thought to herself.

As she walked past the children, DorisEthel saw a big round egg. It was powder blue and lying in a soft fluffy nest in a basket. No one was sitting on it or even paying it any attention so she climbed up and settled herself down. She closed her eyes and was soon fast asleep.

'Hey, chicken,' said a loud voice. It was the children's mother and she was poking DorisEthel with her finger. The children were standing beside her, laughing and pointing.

'Hey, chicken,' said the woman, 'get off my knitting.' She picked up the old chicken and put her down on the grass. The children tickled the top of her head but it didn't seem to feel as good as it usually did and she wandered off into the bushes, clucking to herself. A big black slug was eating its way across a dock leaf right in front of her, but DorisEthel just didn't feel hungry.

'I don't want much out of life,' she muttered to herself as she drifted restlessly round the garden, 'just a dry box, some soft straw and something to hatch. It isn't much to ask.'

She walked past the rabbits and under the tall trees, complaining softly to herself. The other animals called out good mornings as she went by but she didn't seem to notice any of them. She dragged her feet in the earth, looked out across the canal and sighed deeply.

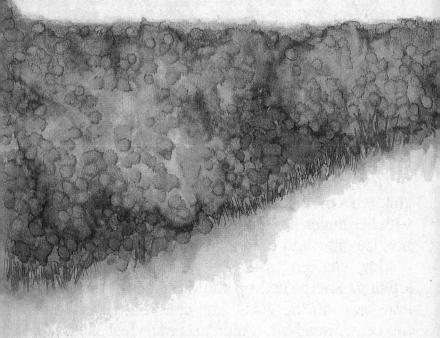

'What's the matter with the old chicken?' they asked, but no one knew.

'I just want an egg to sit on,' said DorisEthel.

'An egg?' said a rabbit. 'You're too old for that sort of thing.'

'Yes,' agreed another. 'You should be enjoying your retirement.'

'Exactly,' said a third. 'You don't want to be thinking about children at your age.'

'It's all very well saying that,' said DorisEthel, 'but you're not a chicken. That's what we do, sit on eggs. That's what we're for.'

As the days went by and the summer grew fuller, DorisEthel got more and more miserable. All around her the other animals had children. Baby rabbits peered out from the safety of their burrow as she went by. Above her in the trees the nests were full of hatching eggs. In curled-up nettle leaves tiny new spiders ate their way to the outside world and in the pond tadpoles wriggled in the sunlight. Even in the old overgrown car by the apple trees there was a nest of young sparrows. It seemed as if the whole world had babies except her.

No one could say anything to get the old chicken out of her mood. As the days went by and the summer grew fuller, she got worse and worse. If she went near anything that was in the slightest bit round she sat on it and tried to hatch it. The garden was soon full of squashed toadstools and polished stones. Whenever she found some dry grass and a few twigs she scraped them up into a nest and sat in the middle of it with her eyes shut. One day as she ambled across the lawn, Elsie the mole popped up from her tunnels and before she could burrow down again DorisEthel sat on her.

'I could have sworn it was morning,' said Elsie as she opened her eyes in total darkness. She thought the sky had fallen down on top of her, but when she realised that the sky smelled of damp chicken she understood what was happening.

'If you don't get off me this minute,' she

shouted, 'I'll bite you.'

'I thought you were an egg,' said DorisEthel as she stood up. 'Sorry.'

'Do I look like an egg?' said Elsie.

'Some days everything looks like an egg,' said DorisEthel. 'And today's one of those days.'

'Stupid chicken,' said Elsie and dived back into her tunnel. She had smelled a big worm thirty feet away and wanted to catch it before it got away.

DorisEthel wandered aimlessly down to the pond and stood ankle deep in the mud at its edge. For half an hour she just stood there, staring into the water. Little creatures wriggled between her toes in the puddle but she didn't notice them.

'Excuse me, mister,' said a voice beside her.

'What?' said Ethel, too depressed to bother telling the owner of the voice that she was a mrs not a mister.

'Is that your mud or can anyone have a go?'

Ethel looked down and saw a huge round toad sitting on a clump of grass, staring at her. She dragged her feet out of the mud and paddled off into the undergrowth.

'Help yourself, warty,' she said.

'Ooh, someone got out of bed the wrong side this morning, didn't they?' said the toad and flung himself into the puddle.

The next morning DorisEthel felt a little better. The children brought her mug of corn before they went off to school and when they tickled her on the head it nearly felt wonderful again. But the broody feeling was still there. Every time she shut her eyes she saw fluffy yellow chicks running round her legs.

'Cuckoos are always on the lookout for some- where to lay their eggs,' said one of the rabbits. 'Why don't you have a word with them? Maybe they'd lay one in your box.'

'What's a cuckoo?' said DorisEthel and the rabbit told her.

'That's awful,' said the old chicken. 'I don't want some horrible bird kicking all my babies out of their nest.'

'You haven't got any babies,' said the rabbit.

'I will have,' said DorisEthel, 'when Eric comes back.'

The rabbit started to say, 'Eric was a casserole years ago,' but she stopped herself and said, 'Oh yes, well, I hadn't thought of that.'

'Well, I'm going back to my box in case Eric comes back while I'm out,' said DorisEthel and walked off. When she got to the lawn she remembered about Eric.

'What a stupid old chicken I am,' she said to herself.

It was Sunday afternoon. The man came out of the house, uncovered a small hole at one side of the lawn, dropped a golf ball at the other and swiped it with a golf club. The ball rolled across the grass and after another couple of taps fell into the hole. He took another golf ball out of his pocket and sent it down the hole after the first one. Over and over again he took the two balls to one side of the lawn and knocked them back into the hole. Two sparrows were sitting in a tree watching him

'What do you think he's doing?' asked the first sparrow.

'I haven't the faintest idea,' said the second. 'But I'd be suprised if they hatch out after the bashing he's given them.'

'Absolutely,' said the first sparrow. 'The shells must be as hard as concrete.'

'Yeah,' said the second, 'and whoever's inside them must have a terrible headache.'

The constant clattering of the golf balls finally woke DorisEthel up. She watched the man put an egg on the grass and bash it with a bent stick. The egg flew across the lawn and vanished and then the man did it again. DorisEthel couldn't believe it. The man had been so kind to her. He'd given her a smart new box to live in and every day his children brought her food. Yet here he was, killing baby chickens.

DorisEthel climbed out of her box and ran onto the lawn, squawking loudly. As a golf ball rolled past her she threw herself on top of it. The man walked over and squatted down beside her, laughing.

'What are you doing, chicken?' he said with a smile. Animals can't understand what humans say any more than humans can understand animals, so DorisEthel just sat there glaring at him.

'Stay there,' said the man. 'I'm going to get my camera.'

43

He got up and went into the house. The minute he was out of sight DorisEthel stood up and pushed and shoved the golf ball until it was hidden in the long grass. By the time the man got back with his camera she had sunk down on top of it, almost out of sight.

'Doris,' called the man, 'where are you?'

He went back into the house to get his family to help him find DorisEthel and while he was gone the old chicken rolled the other ball into her nest.

'An egg,' she murmured to herself, 'and another egg.'

'She's not in here,' said the children, looking in her apple box.

'Five eggs,' whispered DorisEthel who couldn't count.

'She's not in the shed either,' said the woman.

'Seven eggs,' thought DorisEthel.

At last they found her. She sank down as flat as she could, but the man slid his hand underneath her and found the two golf balls. But he didn't take them away because he knew what DorisEthel wanted and the next day he got planks of wood and a roll of felt and mended the old hen house. When it was finished and tight against the wind and rain he filled it with fresh straw and five eggs from a chicken farm. Then he sat DorisEthel in her new nest and gave her a bowl of rice pudding, which was her favourite food.

For almost three weeks DorisEthel sat on the eggs. On good days, the man left the hen house door open and DorisEthel dozed in the sunshine. In the middle of the day when the sun was at its hottest she climbed off the nest and went outside to stretch her legs and eat a few slugs. On wet days she sunk down into the warm straw and listened to the summer rain dancing on the roof. Inside the eggs, life began to stir and DorisEthel could feel the chicks tapping at the shells.

At last the waiting was over and one by one the eggs broke open and once again DorisEthel had fluffy yellow chicks round her feet, looking up at her with love and admiration. And once again she felt loved and important.

'We'll have to find names for them all,' said the little girl.

'Which ones are boys and which ones are girls?' asked her brother, but no one knew.

'Oh well,' said the girl, 'we'll just have to call them all Doris.'

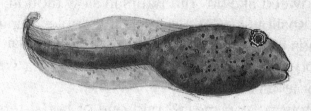

Brenda the Tadpole

It was midday and the sky was blue from side to side. The sunshine shone down into the pond through a colander of leaves. Two moorhens swam around, leaving ripples in the water that carried the light into dark corners at the water's edge. A frog blinked and slipped into the water with a soft splash. Dragonflies, woken by the warmth, flew backwards and forwards along their territories, meeting each other with a fierce clattering of wings before flying on again. Birds came to the edge of the pool to drink and on its surface pondskaters dented the water as they hunted for food.

Below the water was another world, a world hardly touched by wind or rain, a complete universe of tiny jungles and fearsome creatures. Great diving beetles hunted through the roots of water lilies like lions. Newts paddled through the pondweed like tiny dinosaurs in slow motion, and in a shallow sunlit corner new tadpoles hung on clouds of soft green slime.

'Do you like being a tadpole?' asked a young tadpole called Susan.

'How do you mean?' said one of her sisters.

'You know,' said Susan. 'Would you rather be a tadpole or something else?'

'Like what?'

'I dunno,' said Susan.

'A filing cabinet,' said a tadpole called Doreen.

'What's a filing cabinet?' asked Susan.

'It's that brown rusty thing down there in the mud,' said Doreen.

'You don't half talk a load of rubbish, you lot,' said a tadpole called Brenda.

'Oh yes,' said Susan, 'and what amazingly important things have you got to talk about then?'

'Well, what about green slime?' said Brenda. 'That's important.'

'Go on then,' sneered Doreen, 'talk about green slime.'

'Well, it's nice isn't it?' said Brenda.

'Is that it?' asked Susan.

'Er, yes,' said Brenda.

'Great,' said Susan, 'that's really important. Green slime's nice. That's brilliant.'

'Well, what about our mummy?' asked Brenda. 'Why haven't we got a mummy?'

Doreen and Susan and the other tadpoles looked awkward and confused. It was midday and the sun was as high as it could be in the sky. Bright light shone down into the pond, in some places reaching right down to the mud at the bottom. All the tadpoles wriggled nervously in the sun's warmth.

'Of course we've got a mummy,' said Susan. 'We wouldn't be here if we hadn't had a mummy.'

'The water lilies haven't got a mummy,' said Doreen.

'They don't count,' said Susan, 'they're plants.'

'Maybe that's what we are,' said Doreen. 'Plants.'

'Don't be ridiculous,' said Brenda. 'We're animals and as far as I can see, we haven't got a mummy.'

'Or a daddy,' said Doreen.

'We must have,' said Susan.

'Alright,' said Brenda, 'where is she?'

'Maybe she's not in the pond,' said Susan.

'She'd have to be,' said Brenda. 'We can't leave the water, can we?'

The others agreed she was right and so a search was organised. All eighty-seven tadpoles swam round the pond searching for the giant tadpole that would be their mother. An hour later the seventy four that hadn't been eaten gathered together in the cloud of green slime.

'Well,' asked Brenda, 'has anyone seen our mummy?'

'No,' said everyone.

'Me neither,' said Brenda.

'What does our mummy look like?' asked Doreen.

'Like us only bigger, stupid,' said Susan. 'A giant tadpole.'

'How beautiful,' said Doreen, all dreamy-eyed. 'A huge vision of smooth black loveliness.'

'Yes, yes,' said Brenda impatiently. 'Has anyone seen her?'

'No,' said everyone.

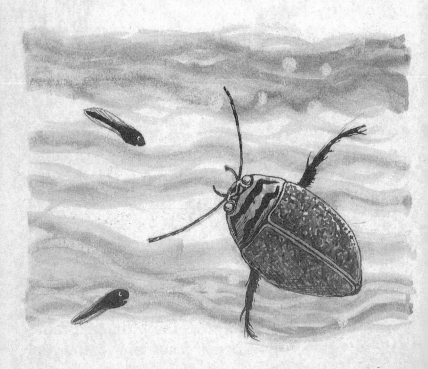

They had seen horrid wriggling things with sharp pincers that had chased them out of the shadows. They had seen shiny black beetles swimming through the tiny seas carrying bubbles of air under their wings. They had seen dragonflies creeping down into the water to lay their eggs, and they had seen a giant green toad all covered in bumps and warts lumbering through the bulrushes. In every place there was life, some so small it could not be seen, but nowhere was there a sign of the giant tadpole that would be their mother.

'Apart from us, everything else in this pond is ugly,' said Doreen.

'Especially the toad,' said Susan.

'Yuk,' said Brenda. 'I don't even want to talk about that disgusting thing, all green and warty.'

'Yeah,' said Susan, 'horrid gherkin face.'

The summer moved slowly on. The giant flowers on the water lilies opened wide and turned their hearts towards the sun. The bulrushes grew taller and taller, casting their shadows longer and longer across the pond and out onto the grass. All day long the air was filled with a haze of flies. Swallows dived down between the trees, catching the flies and dipping their heads in the smooth water. The garden grew fat and lazy. Animals dozed in the midsummer heat of July and those that did move did so with slow deliberation and only in the cool of evening. Under the midday sky, flowers drooped and trickled their pollen into the soft air. It seemed as if everything had slowed down to a complete standstill and the world would stay this way forever.

In the pond, life slowed down too. For weeks the sun had shone down into the clear water until it was as tender as a warm bath. Even the darkest shadows under the lilies were warm, and great clouds of tiny water-fleas swam everywhere. The moorhens' eggs had hatched and as soon as their chicks had been old enough their parents had taken them back to the canal.

In the forest of slime, things were happening to the tadpoles. Their soft black coats of velvet had changed to speckled brown and green and strange things were happening inside them.

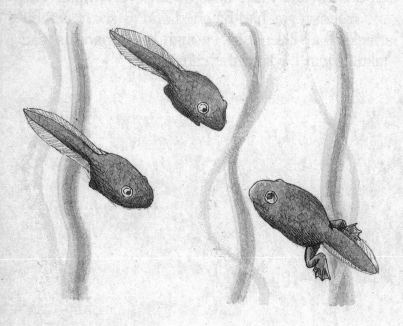

'I don't half feel weird,' said Susan.

'How do you mean?' asked Brenda.

'Well sort of lumpy,' said Susan.

'Do you keep thinking about climbing out of the water?' said Doreen.

'Yes, I do. Do you?' asked Susan.

'Yes,' said Doreen.

'Maybe we're not well,' said Brenda.

'Of course,' said Susan, 'that's it. That's why we're all off colour.'

'I think we've got mumps,' said Doreen. 'That's why we all feel lumpy.'

'It's more than lumps,' said Brenda wriggling out from the leaf she'd been hiding behind. 'It's legs.'

The other tadpoles looked at her and sure enough she had two tiny legs growing out of her. She had shrunk too. Where there had been a long elegant tail Brenda now had a dumpy stump.

'Oh, that's awful,' said Susan, backing away from Brenda. The others did the same and when Brenda stopped nibbling slime and ate a water-flea they all swam off feeling quite sick. But one by one they grew legs and not just two but four, and one by one their tails slowly disappeared and the strangest thing of all was that they all thought they looked rather good.

'My back legs are so big that I can jump right out of the water,' said Doreen.

'My back legs are so big that I can jump right over a mouse,' said Susan.

'Jumping's not so special,' said Brenda. 'Anyone can do that.'

'Oh yes,' said Susan, 'and what amazingly special thing have you got then?'

'Warts,' said Brenda, 'great big wrinkly green warts.'

'So've I,' said Doreen. 'So've I.'

'We all have,' said Susan. 'We're all as warty as toads.'

There was a long silence. The tadpoles stood in the mud, staring at their feet. They looked at each other and realised that they weren't tadpoles any more. They looked at the peaceful green toad all covered in bumps and warts lumbering through the bulrushes, the quiet brown-eyed giant they had called gherkin face, and realised that she was the mother they had all been looking for.

'You know,' said Brenda later that day when they had all crawled under a big wet stone, 'when you look at her closely, she really is incredibly beautiful.'

Geoff the Snail

'Come on, hurry up,' said Geoff the snail. 'If we don't get there soon, someone else will get it.'

'If we don't get there soon,' said his brother John, 'it will have turned into a fossil.'

The two snails were inside a milk bottle where they had been hibernating since the autumn. Early that morning the spring sunshine had shone through the glass until the damp air inside the bottle was as warm as a summer's day. The warmth had woken the two snails from their long sleep and in the grass outside they could see an old brown apple core. This was what they were now trying to reach.

'I'm starving,' said Geoff. 'In fact, I'm so hungry that I can't even remember when I last ate something.'

'That doesn't mean anything,' said John. 'Snails haven't got any memories. If something happened a few minutes ago us snails can't remember it.'

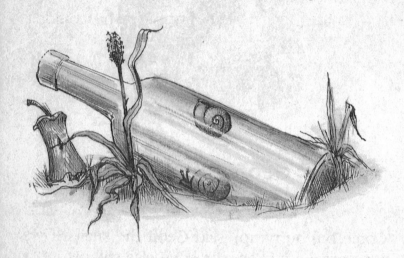

'Remember what?' said Geoff.

'Eh?'

'If I don't get something to eat soon,' said Geoff, 'my shell will fall off and I'll look like a slug.'

'Don't be disgusting,' said John. 'Horrible naked creatures.'

'Where?'

This is one of the reasons that snails are so slow. It isn't just that they move very slowly, but it's also that they keep forgetting why they are moving or where they are moving to.

'It's nice in here, isn't it?' said Geoff.

'Where?' said John.

'Hey, look out there,' said Geoff, 'an apple core.'

By the time John had turned round to look, Geoff had forgotten what it was he was looking at.

'I think I'll go inside my shell for a bit,' he said, and disappeared.

'Who said that?' said John. When he couldn't see anyone he got frightened and went back inside his shell too.

A bit later Geoff stuck his head out and said, 'I'm starving. In fact, I'm so hungry that I can't even remember when I last ate something.'

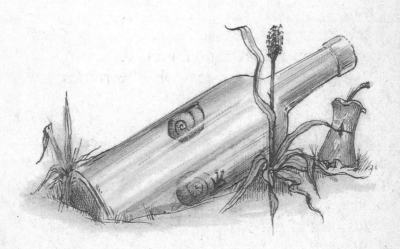

'That doesn't mean anything,' said John, reappearing too. 'Snails haven't got any memories. If something happened a few minutes ago us snails can't remember it.'

By the time they got outside it was raining and the apple core had started growing into a tree.

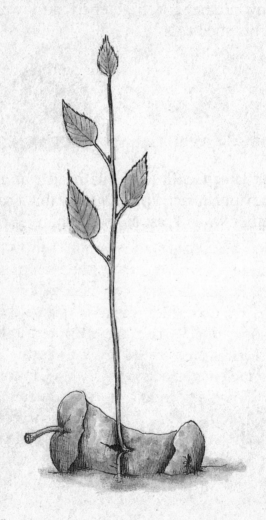

Joan the Sparrow

It was raining everywhere. It was the end of July and the air was warm and heavy. The heat of summer was caught and hemmed in by the rain that came down in heavy sheets. In sheltered places, under leaves and inside the old car, swarms of busy flies sheltered from the storm. Imprisoned by the rain, they hovered in crowded confusion as they waited for it to pass.

The ancient car had stood at the bottom of the garden for thirty years. Its tyres were dull and cracked like the skin of an old rhinoceros and its wheels sunk deep into the ground. Tall grass and weeds grew everywhere, hiding the dark spaces beneath the floor and creeping up inside the engine. For as long as anyone could remember there had been birds nests inside it and in the horse-hair seats there were families of mice. Spiders had laid cobwebs across the steering wheel and in the soft ferns growing on the damp floor was a world of silverfish and centipedes, a small jungle hidden away in a city garden.

Joan the sparrow stood on the back of one of the car seats and picked flies out of the air. There were so many she hardly had to lift a wing to catch them. In the glove compartment of the old car her five chicks were so fat that they were almost falling out of the nest. Their adult feathers were nearly grown and in another few days they would be gone.

Summer had come so early that there would be time for a third brood. Joan had never had three lots of children in one summer before. She had met other sparrows who had, and in fact she had been the child of a third brood herself. The winter had come suddenly that year and her brothers and sisters hadn't survived the cold frosts. Joan had escaped by crawling into the heating vent of a café where she had stayed for three months, living on the fat that had collected on the pipes over the past twenty years. The sun had come out at Christmas and Joan had climbed out of her hideout to find the rest of her family gone.

The rain moved away and Joan flew out of the car into the warm sunshine. Everything was so rich and green that it was almost growing before her eyes. Joan's partner Charlie flew out from the bushes where he had been sheltering and they hopped across the lawn collecting the flies that hadn't survived the storm.

'The children will be off in a couple of days,' said Joan.

'Thank goodness for that,' said Charlie. 'We'll get a bit of peace at last.'

'Well, I had thought we could have a third brood,' said Joan. 'It's only July.'

'Oh, come on,' said Charlie. 'We're just about to get a bit of peace and quiet and you want to start all over again.'

'I know,' said Joan, 'but . . . . '

'It'll be autumn soon,' Charlie added. 'It's time we were fattening ourselves up, never mind another lot of babies.'

'I know, I know.'

But it didn't matter what either of them said, instinct held them in its grasp. They both knew the risks and they knew there wouldn't be a spare moment for the rest of the summer. While all the other animals in the garden were building up their strength for the winter they would be using all theirs raising a new family that would probably be too young to survive the snow. They knew all these things, but it made no difference. They had no choice. Because they could have children, they would have children. That's how nature works. It never leaves any empty spaces. If it did, everything would have died out thousands of years ago.

So a few days later the second lot of chicks flew off into the garden and Charlie cleared out the nest in the old car. When it was ready, Joan laid five more eggs. The days passed and she sat contentedly in the nest. Looking out of the little hole in the side of it she could see the back of the car seat. For fifteen years, since the door had fallen off, the wind and rain had blown into the old car and the seat that had once been bright red leather was now dull brown. There was grass growing in the folds where the leather had split and the mice that had lived inside the seat for generations were thinking of looking for somewhere warmer to live.

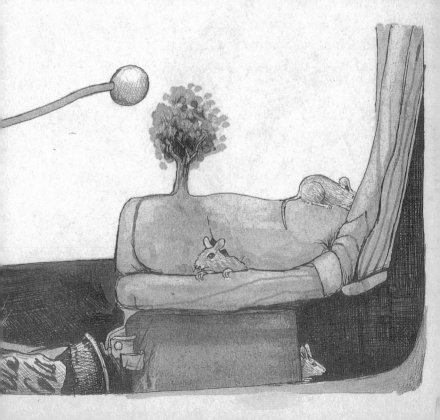

Joan watched for three days while a spider wove a beautiful web between the seat and the glove compartment. Backwards and forwards, over and over again the spider went until she had finished. Then she came to a spot just below Joan's nest and waited for the flies to get caught in her trap. But she didn't get any flies; instead she caught a big fat sparrow called Charlie who swore and cursed as he pulled the cobwebs off his legs. And she also got eaten.

'I'll sit on the eggs for a bit, if you like,' said Charlie, hopping onto the nest.

'Yes, I could do with stretching my wings,' said Joan.

'There's a huge ants' nest down by the pond,' said Charlie, 'and there's loads of slugs on the cabbages.'

Inside their shells the tiny sparrows began to grow. The warm weather went on and on. It looked as if the third brood was going to be a success but then the man decided to move the car.

'Aunty Ferguson used to go to school in that car,' he said to his children. 'We'll take it into the garage and do it up.'

'But it's all rusted away,' said the boy.

'And the door's fallen off,' said the girl.

'And there's a garden growing inside it,' said the woman.

'We can fix all that,' said the man. 'When we've finished, it'll look like new.'

So they chopped down the weeds and bushes that had grown up round the car and propped it up on blocks of wood while they fitted new tyres and poured oil on the wheels. The children searched through the grass and found all the bits that had fallen off and carried them up to the house. Inside her nest, Joan sat as still as midsummer's night while Charlie flew from branch to branch round the apple trees complaining loudly, but everyone was too busy with the car to notice him.

When the wheels were fixed they lowered the car to the ground and inch by inch pushed it slowly across the vegetable garden towards the garage at the side of the house. They rolled the car right across the vegetable beds, digging up carrots and cabbages as they went until they reached the back of the garage.

When the car had been taken down to the bottom of the garden all those years before, there had been a flat lawn next to the garage. Now there were tall trees growing there with no way through.

'Well, we're not cutting the trees down,' said the man. 'We'll have to make a hole in the back of the garage.'

They took out the window in the back wall and got hammers and chisels and knocked out enough bricks to get the old car into the garage. When it was safely inside, they put all the bricks and the window back again and only then did they notice the two sparrows.

Charlie had followed the car into the garage and while the man had been cementing the bricks into place, he had sat up in the roof. Only when the window had been put in did the bird panic and flutter against the glass, but when the boy opened the window Charlie didn't fly out. Instead he flew inside the front of the car and then the children saw Joan sitting on her nest.

They left the window open so Joan and Charlie could come and go as they wanted. When the eggs hatched they were back and forwards all day long fetching food for the new chicks. The man, who liked to take life easy, was happy for an excuse to leave the car alone for a while. The children thought it was wonderful that a family of birds was actually living in part of their house.

When autumn came and the air grew cool the family of sparrows stayed safe and warm in their new home. Each day the children brought them food so that when the cold snows came they didn't have to go outside at all. The next spring when life began again they flew out into the world fat and healthy and happy.

Inside the garage the man blew the dust off his spanners and set to work on the car. It took him six years to finish it and all that time the sparrows' nest stayed where it was and every summer Joan laid three lots of eggs in it.

'You always said you wanted to move,' said Charlie as they sat in an apple tree looking down at the yellow patch of grass where the car had been.

'So I did,' said Joan, 'so I did.'

Dennis the Owl

There were seven large oak trees in the back garden and three more in the front. They were the oldest living things in the street and towered over everything, each one like a small forest in whose branches and leaves birds and squirrels and other creatures lived their lives. The trees had been there two hundred years before there had been any houses, and the oldest house was over a hundred years old. In one of the great oaks there were owls. They had lived there since the trees had been big enough to give them homes.

Owls are proud and dignified birds, as majestic as oak trees themselves. Silent and sleeping during the day, at night they glide like soft ghosts through the darkness, hunting small creatures that hurry across open fields and quiet hedgerows. Other animals keep away from owls and treat them with respect.

The two children who had come to live at fourteen had built their tree-house in one of the oaks and in another close by lived Dennis the owl. At least, when he could find the right tree, he lived there. Quite often he would come back at dawn and land on the wrong tree. He would swoop down through the wrong branches and smash the top of his head into the wrong trunk, exactly in the place where the hole he lived in should have been.

'Someone's stolen my house again,' he would say as the stars spun round in his head. 'You go out to get your dinner, not wanting to bother anyone, and while you're out someone steals your house.'

If the weather was warm he would just stay where he was and if it was cold he would flutter unsteadily down to the old car and sleep on the back seat. Sometimes as he sat there it would start raining and he would wake up with water running down his neck and wonder what he was doing wrong.

'I'm sure life should be better than this,' he said to no one. 'All I want is a warm place to sleep and a nice soft mouse for supper. And people to stop hiding my house. And crunchy moths for breakfast and warm slugs for tea.'

'And a friend.'

'And a dry neck.'

The trouble was that Dennis wasn't a proud and dignified bird. He was lost and lonely and not very clever. Nature seemed to have only a certain amount of brains to give out and by the time Dennis had hatched his three sisters had got them all and there was none left for him.

79

'Better to have a kind heart,' his mother used to say, ' than be as clever as . . .'

'As clever as an owl,' said his sisters, laughing and pointing at him.

'. . and have nobody love you,' continued his mother.

He was all alone now. His mother had gone a long time ago and so had his sisters. On still summer nights he sometimes thought he could hear the hooting of another owl far away but he had never seen one.

'What use is a kind heart,' he said to himself, 'if no one knows you've got one?'

Most of the time it was all right, he just got on with things. His house was quite often in the right place. He found plenty of slugs and bits and pieces to eat and he didn't think about anything. Sometimes though, there were dark days when the sun refused to shine in the sky or in his head. On those days he sat in the shadows of his home, unable to move. Sadness wrapped him up in its arms and filled him with a terrible loneliness.

'All I want . . . ,' he said to himself, but he didn't know what it was.

'All I want is something.'

The mood would pass and the next night he
would be out at dusk with a huge appetite,
searching up and down the towpath for mice. In
his whole life he had never caught a mouse. The
mice had soon realised that Dennis was not like
other owls. They realised that they were much
cleverer than he was and, although they could
never hope to be able to run fast enough if he
swooped down on them, they could still stop him
eating them.

One would keep watch and as soon as Dennis
approached he would shout, 'TSP ALERT,' at the
top of his voice. The mice called him TSP which
stood for Two Short Planks.

'Because that's what he's as thick as,' they said.

As Dennis swooped, the mice rolled onto their backs, tucked up their legs and sang:

> 'We are just potatoes.
> Cut us into strips,
> Fry us in a pan
> And make us into chips.'

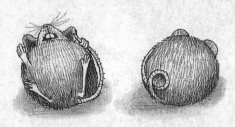

'You look like mice to me,' said Dennis.
'No, no,' sang the mice:

> 'We really are potatoes.
> Boil us in a pan,
> Mash us up with butter
> And eat us with some ham.'

'Potatoes can't speak,' said Dennis, feeling a bit unsure of himself.

'For goodness sake,' sang the mice:

> 'Listen stupid Owl.
> You wearing earplugs?
> We're all just round potatoes.
> Fly off and eat some slugs.'

And that was what poor Dennis did. Every night he shuffled around under the bushes scraping up the grass like an old chicken and eating slugs and beetles. It was no life for an owl. His feathers were broken and muddy, his claws were worn down and his back ached from all the bending over. There were thousands of slugs, but no matter how many he ate, part of him always felt empty. As the sun began to rise he went back to home to bed and wondered if it would be like this for ever.

His sleep was full of dreams of when he had been young, of the long summer after his sisters had gone and he had had his mother all to himself. The days were full of sunshine pouring into the warm nest inside the tree. He sank into the soft feathers and moss and slept until evening. When it was dark his mother flew in and fed him with soft strips of meat and sweet moths. Like the best summers of childhood, it had seemed to go on for ever and ever. Now it was all just a fuzzy memory.

When the people had arrived it had hardly affected Dennis. The crows had come to live in the trees after they had been pushed out of the chimneys and it had become a lot noiser. The children had built a wooden house in the next tree, but none of it had made much difference to the lonely owl. By the time he came out at night, the children were back indoors and the crows were fast asleep. The rest of the animals in the garden generally ignored him. Most of them were asleep too and the other night creatures were too busy making their own livings to be bothered with a miserable owl.

He had tried talking to other animals, but they didn't want to know. He tried hanging round outside the rabbit warren at the bottom of the garden but the rabbits just thought he was trying to eat their babies and slipped out of the back door. He tried talking to the hedgehogs but they were making so much noise crashing through the grass and sucking snails out of their shells that they didn't hear him. He even tried talking to the sparrow that was nesting in the old car, but she sank down into the darkness and pretended she wasn't there.

'All I want is a friend,' said Dennis. 'It doesn't even have to be a special friend, just someone who will talk to me.'

'I'd just like to be a little bit important to someone,' he said to no one.

There were wild cats across the canal in the derelict factories but when Dennis went near them they hissed and spat at him and cut the air with their claws. An ordinary owl who caught mice and screeched at the moon wouldn't have been scared of cats, but Dennis was a gentle soul and even the kittens chased him away. The foxes that lived along the canal pretended he wasn't there.

In his whole life only one animal, apart from his mother, had been kind to him, and that had been an old horse. One moonlit night a barge had tied up at the bottom of the garden. The giant horse that pulled it stood silently under the overhanging branches of the oak trees. The round windows of the boat glowed yellow like a row of pale suns and thin smoke trickled up into the cloudless sky, making a pale ribbon across the moon. Dennis flew down to the fence by the towpath. He had never seen a horse before.

'Hello,' he said.

'Hello,' said the horse.

'*You're* not a potato, are you?' said Dennis. The horse took a few steps backwards.

'Er, no,' said the horse. And realising Dennis was a bit strange he added. '*You're* not are you?'

'No,' said Dennis. 'I'm an owl.'

'Yes,' said the horse, 'I thought you were.'

'Well, you were right,' said Dennis. In the bushes behind him there was a crashing sound as three young rabbits fell laughing off the pile of twigs they had climbed up. The horse leant down and took a mouthful of grass. Dennis sat on the fence and watched him. An hour later the horse was still eating grass and Dennis was still watching him.

'Did you want something?' asked the horse.

'Well, I was wondering,' said Dennis, 'if you'd be my friend.'

'Mmm,' said the horse, 'I'm actually a bit busy at the moment.'

'Well, when you're not busy,' said Dennis. 'How about then?'

'All right then,' said the horse. 'Come back tomorrow'. But tomorrow never came, for the next night the barge and the horse were twenty miles away and Dennis never saw them again.

And then his whole life changed.

One night the man was driving home down country lanes. The rain threw itself out of the sky in a violent summer thunderstorm and as the car went round a bend the man saw something flapping in the middle of the road. He stopped and in the headlights' beam he saw a bird with a broken wing. It was struggling towards the side of the road, dragging its wing through the crashing rain.

The man got out of the car and wrapped the bird up in his coat. It was a wild-eyed owl and although he was rescuing it, it tried to attack the man as he carried it back to his car. He laid it on the back seat and went home.

For the next few weeks the injured owl lived in the garage. It hid away in the darkness up in the beams of the roof staring down at its rescuers with wild yellow eyes. The vet came and mended its wing but it was never able to fly again. It looked down at the food the children brought but only when they had gone and it was quiet again would it flutter down to eat. Even after a month when all its bones were mended and the feathers it had lost were growing back again, it wouldn't let any of the family go near it.

'She can live in the garden,' said the man. 'And we'll have to feed her for the rest of her life.'

'She can live in our tree house,' said the boy and that's what she did. They filled in the sides that faced into the wind and made a perch from a broom handle. And when everything was ready and she had her bandages removed, the man put on a pair of thick gloves and carried her up the ladder to her new home. They tethered her to the perch to stop her falling out of the tree until she got used to it and went back into the house.

'Maybe she'll get better one day,' said the boy, 'and fly away.'

'I think we'll call her Audrey,' said the girl.

Audrey sat on her perch looking out into the twilight. It was the middle of June and below her in an apple tree a blackbird was singing its summer song. The bats were up and about, swooping in and out of the trees chasing flies.

'I wonder what they taste like,' thought Audrey. 'Bats that is, not flies.'

They flew so fast that she had never caught one and she certainly wasn't going to now.

If she stretched her legs and leant right forward, she could see right down to the ground below. A hedghog was drinking at the edge of a little pond. Audrey had to drink out of a tin cup.

'If the man hadn't picked me up,' she thought, 'I wouldn't be drinking out of a tin cup.'

She thought back to the night of the storm. She had been hunting far away from home when it had started and in her rush to get back she had flown straight into a telephone wire and broken her wing. She thought of her home in the sycamore tree in the middle of a large wood, and as she sat there day-dreaming she almost missed the black

shape flying right in front of her. It was silhouetted across the evening sky, a shape just like her own.

'Hey,' she shouted and the shape crashed into a tree.

'Ow,' said a voice in the darkness.

'Over here,' she called.

'Where?'

This went on for a while, but at last Dennis stood on the edge of the tree house looking at Audrey.

'You're an owl,' he said.

'Well, I'm not a potato,' said Audrey.

'I can see that,' said Dennis, 'you haven't got any fur or paws.'

'What?' said Audrey.

'Well . . ' Dennis started to explain.

'It's alright,' said Audrey, 'don't tell me.'

'Will you be my friend?' said Dennis.

Audrey looked over the edge of the tree-house and said, 'See those little furry things running round down there?'

'Yes,' said Dennis, 'the potatoes.'

'Er, yes,' said Audrey, 'the potatoes. Well if you go and get me one of those, I'll be your friend.'

'Alright.'

Dennis flew down and although the mice rolled up as small as they could and sang every song they knew, it did no good. Dennis had a friend and his friend liked potatoes.

A week later the man took the tether off

Audrey's leg and, although she never flew properly again, she hopped and fluttered from branch to branch through the great oak trees. And in the spring she fluttered into Dennis's nest and laid four eggs and a month later he had four more friends and was so busy catching potatoes that he never had time to be lonely again.

Metamorphosis

Beneath green leaves,
In hard cocoons,
In tunnels damp and cold,
Nature's heat turns night to day,
Rebuilds the tired and old.

She holds the thing
So small and drab
In the focus of her eye,
Takes ashes from a fading fire
And builds a butterfly.

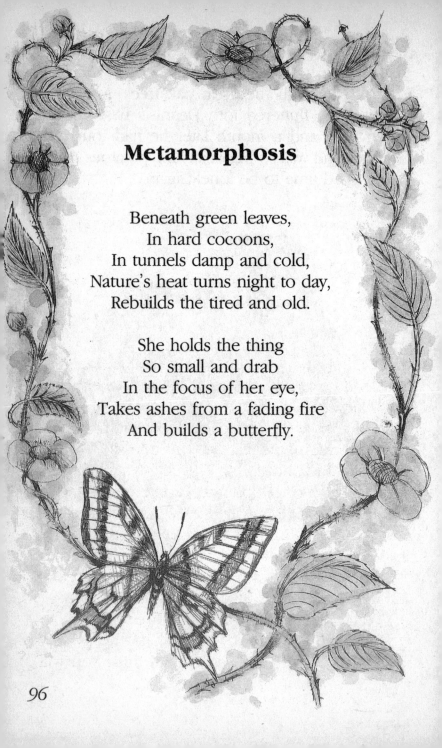

The Five Dorises

DorisEthel the chicken was teaching her five chicks how to catch worms. She had taken them to a newly-dug bed of earth in the vegetable garden where she scratched about with her feet and then jumped back, head to one side, to see what she had uncovered. The chicks were bored. They had all the food they wanted brought to them by the children and they couldn't see the point of grubbing about in a load of mud. They had scraped up a row of radishes and wanted to do something else.

'Mum,' said Doris One, 'can we go and play?'

'Yeah, mum,' said Doris Four, 'we're fed up.'

'Listen children,' said DorisEthel, 'this is very important. It's the most important thing you will ever learn.'

'What, rummaging about in the earth for those horrible worm things?' asked Doris Two.

'Yes,' said DorisEthel, 'it's what chickens do. All over the world there are chickens scraping up the dirt and eating worms and slugs.'

'Well, I'm not going to,' said Doris Three. 'I'm going to eat porridge.'

'Me too,' said Doris Five.

'And us,' said the other three Dorises.

'And cake,' said Doris Three. 'Don't forget the cake we got last Sunday.'

DorisEthel could see that she was wasting her time. The chicks were in an awkward mood and no amount of talking would make them change their mind. Maybe she was old-fashioned but she could think of nothing more wonderful than pulling a big wet worm out of the soft earth and feeling it wriggle down your throat as you swallowed it.

'Children today,' she sighed, and waddled off across the lawn towards the house.

'Cake indeed,' she said. 'What's the world coming to? When I was their age we had to eat secondhand caterpillars and newspapers.'

'Mind you,' she thought to herself, 'it was nice cake, especially the raisins all slimy in the middle like slugs.'

'What are we going to do now?' said Doris One as the chicks rushed after the old hen.

'Play,' asked Doris Two.

'Go on then,' said Doris Four, 'do it.'

'Do what?' said Doris Two.

'Play.'

'Er, right then,' said Doris Two, 'come on.' She scuttled up the back door step and wriggled through the cat flap into the house. The four other chicks ran after her, landing one after the other on the mat. DorisEthel tried to get through the flap after her children but she was too fat. She paced up and down outside the door clucking loudly and calling them. Inside, the five chicks pretended they couldn't hear her. They stood in the middle of the kitchen floor and looked around.

'Is this playing, then?' said Doris Three.

'Yes,' said Doris Two.

'It's great isn't it?' said Doris Five.

'What are we going to do now?' said Doris One.

'We could eat the cat food,' said Doris Three.

'Cat food?' said Doris Four nervously. 'Do you mean there's a cat in here?'

'Well, if there's a cat flap, there must be a cat,'

said Doris Three.

'What, a big cat with teeth and claws and stuff?' asked Doris Four.

'Errr, yes,' said Doris Three, looking round.

'I want my mummy,' cried Doris Four, running back to the door. The other chicks rushed after her and they all collided in a great heap on the mat.

'Mum, mum,' she cried as they scrambled out into the garden, 'there's a giant cat after us.'

'It's going to eat us all up,' said Doris Three.

The five chicks ran as fast they could across the lawn and back into the hen house. DorisEthel, who knew there wasn't a cat in the house, waddled slowly after them. Inside the hut, all the chicks jumped into the nesting box and hid in the straw, except Doris Four who jumped on top of the box and pretended to be brave.

'Cock-a-doodle,' she shouted.

'Who said that?' said DorisEthel as she came into the hut.

'It wasn't me,' said Doris Three.

'It wasn't us,' said Doris One and Doris Five.

'Said what?' asked Doris Two.

'That cock-a-doodle noise,' said DorisEthel.

'Sorry, mum,' said Doris Four. 'It just sort of came over me.'

'Do you know what it means?' said DorisEthel.

'No. I don't even know why I said it,' said Doris Four.

'Is it rude?' said Doris Three. The four chicks in the nest box started sniggering and nudging each other.

'It's rude. It's rude,' they chorused.

'No it isn't,' said DorisEthel. 'It means that Doris Four is a boy.'

The four chicks in the nest box giggled even more.

'No I'm not,' said Doris Four, 'I'm a chicken.'

'Yes, of course you are,' said DorisEthel, 'but you're a boy chicken. You're a cockerel.'

The other four Dorises jumped out of the nest box and stared up at Doris Four. He looked very confused and shuffled off to the back where they couldn't see him. But a cockerel he was and there was no getting away from it.

'I don't want to be a boy,' he said. 'I won't say it any more.' But he couldn't stop himself. He felt the words coming up inside him and he clenched his little beak shut as tight as he could but he just couldn't stop them.

'COCK-A-DOODLE-DOO!' he shouted at the top of his tiny voice.

'Wow,' said Doris Three, 'that was great.'

Her sisters thought it was great too, but no one thought it was as great as DorisEthel did. She fluffed her feathers out with pride. Over the summer, Doris Four grew into a magnificent cockerel and once again the days began with a great crowing as he stood proud and tall on the shed roof and woke the sleeping world. And once again, like Eric before him, he got soaked to the skin as next door's upstairs window opened and a bucketful of water came flying out.

Doris Four's sisters had grown up too and were laying eggs every day. The hen house was a constant bustle with clucking and crowing and the children forever in and out. It was all too much for DorisEthel, so she went back to the peace and quiet of her apple box to dream of days gone by when she too had been part of it all.

106

'If he's a cockerel,' said the boy, 'we can't call him Doris any more.'

'We'll call him Kevin,' said the little girl.

'No, no,' said the boy. 'We'll call him Boris.'

And that's what they did, though to his sisters and DorisEthel he was always known as DorisBoris.

Arnold the Mouse

As night fell over the quiet streets, the animals that slept through the day began to wake up. In dark tunnels and soft nests, creatures stirred and opened their eyes. They stretched their legs and wings, tasted the evening air and thought of breakfast.

For a few it would be the last night of their lives. Hedgehogs, blinded by two suns, would be squashed by cars. Mice, racing across open lawns, would be food for cats and owls. But for most of the animals, living by night was safer than living by day. In the darkness they could slip into places unseen and while the rest of the world slept they could live their lives in peace.

As the sky disappeared, the rabbits came out of

their burrows. With eyes still full of sleep, they sniffed the fresh air and spread out across the garden and canal bank. They crept into next door's garden and ate their way along the neat rows of flowers. The nervous man and his thin wife put wire netting along the fence but the rabbits just went underneath it. On warm summer evenings, next door's cat sat on the patio and watched them. The moles burrowed under the lawn and threw up piles of earth on to the neatly clipped grass, and on calm nights spiders spun their webs between tall grass and low branches.

This night was a calm night. It was so quiet that Arnold the mouse could hear the traps going off in the other houses along the street. He rolled over in his nest of newspaper under the kitchen floor and a shiver ran down his back as he thought of his fellow mice coming to such a violent end.

There were no traps in his house; at least, not the steel spring type that killed you. In his house the trap was a warm and welcoming plastic box and inside it was a piece of fabulous cheese. Every night Arnold crept into the trap and ate the cheese. And every night he tripped over the bar and the door fell shut behind him. Twenty-two times he had done it and twenty-two times at eight o'clock in the morning the man had carried the trap down to the bottom of the garden and tipped Arnold out through a gap in the hedge onto the canal bank. It was the same every day. Arnold knew the routine so well that if he ran as fast as possible he could be back in the house before the man was.

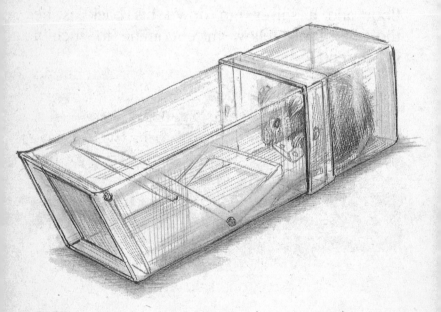

On the twenty-third day the man said, 'I'm sure that's the same mouse we caught yesterday.'

'Brilliant,' thought Arnold. 'I'm sharing my home with an idiot.'

The children peered through the brown plastic at Arnold and asked, 'How can you tell?'

'Great,' thought Arnold. 'They're all idiots.'

'Isn't it incredible?' he said to his wife, Edna, when he was back under the kitchen floor for the twenty-fourth time. 'I can understand how maybe they can't tell each other apart. I mean, all humans look the same, but how on earth they can't see it's me every time, is beyond me.'

'They're idiots,' said Edna.

'That's what I reckon,' said Arnold.

The twenty-fifth time, the man tipped Arnold out into his hand and tried to paint a red spot on his fur. Arnold bit the man on the thumb and the man dropped him on the floor. Arnold ran under the kitchen units and back into his nest. The twenty-sixth time, the man put a big thick pair of gloves on and Arnold ended up with a red blob on his head. The next night, just to confuse the man, Edna went in the trap.

'Arnie, you're wicked, you are,' she said to Arnold when she came back from the bottom of the garden the next morning, 'taking advantage of simple people like that.'

Arnold thought of bringing all his friends and relations in and getting them to go into the trap one by one, but he didn't like the idea of giving up his nightly meal of cheese and the next night he went back in the trap.

'Look,' cried the man, 'it *is* the same mouse.'

'The bottom of the garden's not far enough away,' said the woman. 'You'll have to take it right down the street.'

'But it might get run over,' said the man.

'Well, tip it out into someone's garden,' said the woman. 'It can go and bother them.'

The man went to the end of the short street and when no one was looking tipped Arnold over the hedge into the last garden. Arnold had been there many times before. In fact, he had relatives who lived there. So he dusted himself off and ran along behind the fences following the man back home.

'I hope this isn't going to become a habit,' he said when he was back in the kitchen again.

'It's the cheese that's a habit,' said Edna. 'If you stopped going after the cheese you wouldn't keep getting caught.'

'I like cheese,' said Arnold.

'Like cheese!' said Edna. 'It's a bit more than like, isn't it? You're a cheeseaholic.'

'No I'm not,' said Arnold. 'I'm just very fond of a bit of cheese.'

'All right then,' said Edna. 'Let's see. When he puts the trap down tonight, don't go in it.'

'Alright, then.'

'I bet you can't do it,' said Edna. 'I bet you can't stay out of the trap all night.'

'Of course I can, it's easy,' said Arnold. 'What do you bet me?'

'Whatever you like,' said Edna.

'Alright,' said Arnold. 'I bet you a piece of Wensleydale.'

'See,' said Edna, 'all you can think about is cheese.'

And she was right. Before he went to bed, the man put the trap in the kitchen cupboard. Inside it was a delicious, ripe, sweating piece of Stilton. Its powerful, thrilling perfume filled the whole room. Arnold buried his head in the nest but he could still smell it. He tried to sleep but it was impossible. At midnight he went out into the garden to find something else to eat and to get away from the beautiful temptation; but it was useless, he couldn't get it out of his mind.

He went for a run along the towpath. He ran and ran until the house was miles behind him and his lungs were thumping like a tiny steam engine. But no matter what he did, it was no good. Every time he blinked he could see the open door of the trap in his mind and glowing in its heart like a piece of the moon was the pale, irresistible cheese. The new day was hiding just below the horizon and Arnold knew that if he didn't get home before it was light, something with sharp claws would have him for breakfast.

'I could stay here,' he said to himself. 'Hide in a dark hole until tomorrow night and then go home.' But he knew he wouldn't. He knew he would go home and he knew he would go into the trap and eat the cheese. Edna was right, and he'd known it all along.

So, as the sun crept up into the sky and the early birds flew down to catch the worms, Arnold crawled wearily back through the fence at the bottom of the garden, crossed the lawn and slipped into the house. Edna was sitting by the trap waiting for him.

'I tried,' he said. 'I really did.'

'I know, I saw you,' said Edna as Arnold walked into the trap and the door dropped shut behind him.

'It's come back,' said the man. 'That wretched mouse has come back again.'

'You'll have to take it somewhere in the car,' said the woman. 'Drive out into the country and stick it under a bush.'

'Do you think it will be all right?' said the man.

'Of course it will,' said the woman. 'There are hundreds of mice in the country. It'll go and live with them.'

She didn't know that the other mice wouldn't accept Arnold, that every time he tried to go into their homes they would drive him out. So the man put the trap on the back seat of the car and set off for the country.

They drove for miles and miles until they left the last house behind and were surrounded by moonlit fields. In a quiet lane by some trees, the man knelt down in the grass and opened the trap. Arnold looked out and refused to leave. The man pulled the back off the trap and pushed Arnold out with his finger. Then he got back in the car and drove away.

Arnold ran deep into the grass until he found a small dark place to hide. All day he lay there, curled up into a small pathetic ball. In his heart he felt a hopeless loneliness and in his mind a lifeless nothing. He knew he had lost Edna and the perfect garden forever. He had grown up there and so had his parents before him and now it was all gone because of his weakness.

'I wish I was dead,' he thought. 'I am such a pathetic creature.'

When night fell he walked out into the moonlight into a wide open space and waited for an owl to swoop down and end his miserable life. But no owl came and by three o'clock in the morning Arnold was stiff and hungry.

'Maybe if I sit here long enough,' he thought, 'I'll catch a cold and die.'

By five o'clock it was light and suddenly Arnold felt frightened and ran back to the safety of the dark hole. As he ran in, he tripped over a hazelnut that had fallen from the tree above. When an owl hadn't got him and it had been too warm to catch cold, he had thought of starving himself to death. But he hadn't eaten for nearly twenty-four hours and had such a tummyache that he sat down and ate the hazelnut.

'I'm so pathetic,' he said to himself as he fell asleep, 'that I can't do anything right.' And in his dreams he was running down a hill with a giant round cheese rolling after him. Just as he reached the safety of a gate he tripped and fell and the cheese rolled right over him and covered him from head to tail in red wax.

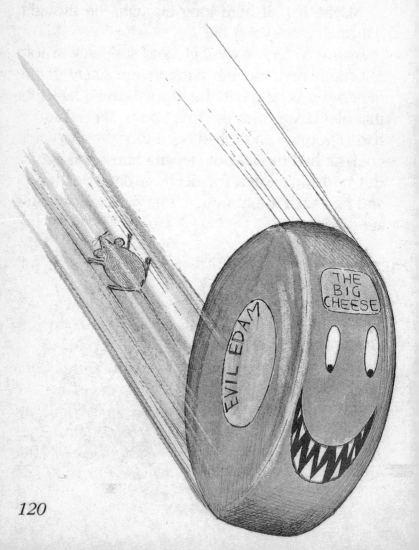

Back at the house, Edna was more angry that sad. Her stupid Arnold had lost everything through no-one's fault but his own. She had done her best to keep him out of the trap but nothing she had said had stopped him. He deserved everything that had happened to him.

'All the same,' she said to her sister Janet, 'I do miss him.'

'You're better off without him,' said Janet.

'You're probably right,' said Edna. 'But I miss him something awful.'

'You'll find someone else. Just wait and see,' said Janet. She was losing patience with Edna and went off into the garden to catch slugs.

'I don't want anyone else,' said Edna, 'I just want my Arnie.'

Then she had an idea. It wasn't a great idea but it was the only one she had and besides, she had nothing to lose. All her children had grown up and gone away. She had nothing to stay in the kitchen for, so she might as well try it.

'If I keep going into the trap,' she said to Janet, 'maybe they'll take me to the same place they took Arnie.'

'That's a ridiculous idea,' said Janet, but Edna had made up her mind and every night for the next week she went and ate the cheese and got caught. The humans weren't very bright. They didn't take her to the country straight away. After six days they painted a red spot on her back and on the seventh day the man took her to the end of the street.

'It isn't going to work,' said Janet. 'You're just wasting your time.' But she wasn't, because on the eighth day the man and the woman got in the car and drove her out into the country. They stopped the car, opened the trap and Edna ran off deep into the grass until she found a small dark place to hide.

It was warm in the dark place and the air was filled with the smell of damp fur and hazelnuts. Something was snoring at the back of the hole and Edna tip-toed nervously into the darkness. Towards the back it was so dark she couldn't see. She walked blindly forward, tripped over a broken nut shell and went flying. She landed on something soft and hairy that wriggled and swore at her.

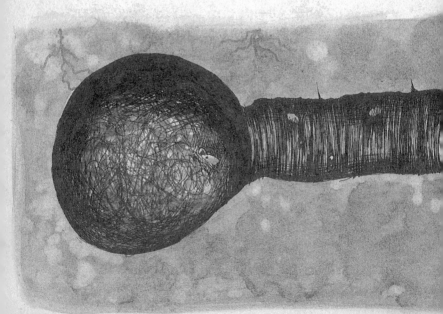

'Arnie?' she said. 'Is that you?'

'Edna?' said the soft hairy thing, 'Is that *you*?'

And of course it was. It was both of them and, although they never went back to the perfect garden, and although there were no more meals of Stilton, they both lived happily ever after.

A year later people came and had a picnic under the hazel tree and when they had gone there was a cheese sandwich left behind. Old dreams came back into Arnold's head, dreams that had gone to sleep. He nibbled away the bread and there it was, a thick slice of cheddar; but when he tasted it, the magic had faded.

'I wonder what I ever saw in it,' he said, and later that night a passing fox picked up the sandwich and took it away.

Attila the Bluebottle

There are times when life is perfect. For Attila the bluebottle it was one of those times. When he actually thought about it, every single day of his life had been perfect and he had been alive for a whole week.

He had spent the morning inside a fish head at the bottom of the dustbin and was so full up he could hardly move. Everywhere he looked it was the same view of paradise. Fat lazy bluebottles full of rotten fish staggered around with big contented grins on their faces.

'I'm so full,' said Attila, 'that if you gave me a rat covered in slime I wouldn't be able to eat a mouthful.'

'I'm so full,' said his sister Lucille, 'that if the rat

covered in slime had been lying at the bottom of a sewer for a year, I wouldn't be able to eat half a mouthful.'

'I'm so full . . . ,' said Attila.

'OK, OK,' said their mother, 'we get the picture.'

'Here,' said Attila, 'do you want to hear a joke?'

'Yeah, go on then,' said Lucille.

'This isn't the Only Joke, is it?' said their mother.

'No, no,' said Attila, 'I just made it up.'

'Go on then,' said their mother.

'Right. Two flies are standing on a dead dog . . .'

'That's brilliant,' said Lucille.

'That's not it,' said Attila. 'I haven't finished.'

'It is the Only Joke,' said his mother. 'I know it is.'

'Go on, go on,' said Lucille.

'Two flies are standing on a dead dog and one says to the other – "Is that your dead dog?"

'Yeah, go on,' said Lucille, hopping about on all her feet.

'And the other fly says . . .'

'. . . No, just carrion,' said their mother with a sigh.

'Oh mum,' said Attila.

'I don't get it,' said Lucille.

While Attila explained the joke to Lucille, their mother beat her head against the rotten fish until she was sick.

'Hey mum, that's brilliant,' said Attila. 'Can you show us how to do that?'

'Oh go and stick your head in a disinfectant bottle,' said his mother and went off to the other side of the dustbin. When she got there, she wriggled though the rubbish until she found a green pork chop. Then she laid six hundred eggs.

'What's the matter with her?' asked Lucille.

'Dunno,' said Attila, 'maybe she's got no sense of humour.'

126

Someone lifted the lid and emptied a bucket of slops into the dustbin. The falling rubbish flattened some of the flies and sent dozens of others buzzing up into the air. Attila and Lucille had been skiing inside the fish head and when the lid had been put back on they crawled out to inspect the latest delivery.

'Yuk,' said Lucille, 'it's all bits of vegetables and fruit peelings.'

'Isn't there any meat at all?' asked Attila.

'Can't see any.'

'What about fish?'

'No.'

'Cheese rind?'

'No,' said Lucille, 'nor jam. It's all just tea bags and cabbage leaves.'

'You know what this means, don't you?' said Attila.

'No.'

'It means they've turned vegetarian,' said Attila. 'It's the end of civilisation as we know it.'

'What are we going to do?' said Lucille.

'We'll have to go somewhere else I suppose.'

'What do you mean?' said Lucille.

'You know,' said Attila, 'move.'

'What, like mum,' said Lucille, 'over behind the dirty nappy mountain?'

'No, no,' said Attila, 'right away.'

'What, as far as the lake of slime, right at the bottom of the dustbin?' said Lucille.

'Further than that,' said Attila, 'right out of the dustbin, into Nowhere.'

'You're mad, you are,' said Lucille. 'We can't live out there.'

'Yes we can. Where do you think we came from in the first place?'

'The Big Fish,' said Lucille. 'We came from inside The Big Fish.'

'No, no,' said Attila, 'where did flies come from before that?'

'I don't understand,' said Lucille.

Attila couldn't think of the right words to say. He wasn't even sure there were any right words; but the one thing he was sure of was that if they didn't leave, they would starve. Lucille understood this and although she was terrified she waited with Attila under the rim and the next time the lid was lifted they flew out into Nowhere.

Inside the dustbin it had always been damp and cool. It had always been dark too, except when the sky lifted and more food fell in. Then there had been a flash of brilliant light like an exploding sun.

Now it was all brilliant light. At first Attila and Lucille were completely blinded. They flew frantically upwards, expecting to hit something at any moment, but there was nothing there. As their eyes became accustomed to the sunshine, they saw the roof of the house below them and flew down to the sea of grey slates and rested. Far below them, a child had just put the dustbin lid back and was going into the house.

'Is this heaven then?' said Lucille nervously.

'I don't think so,' said Attila. 'I think you have to be dead to go to heaven and I don't think we are.'

Flies don't live long enough to sit and think about things too much. It's light, it's dark. It's hot, it's cold. This rat's leg tastes delicious. They never have to think about money or clean shoes. Life for flies is very simple. Attila and Lucille's mother had told them that the inside of the dustbin was the whole universe and they had believed her. After all, it was obvious, the inside of the dustbin was all they could see.

But now they were outside and they could see a lot more. They could see that their dustbin was just one small space in one small garden and that each house down the street had a dustbin of its own.

'So much for listening to mum,' said Attila.

'Yeah,' said Lucille, 'what did she know. She was only two weeks older than us.'

'Two weeks is a long time,' said Attila. 'It's nearly a lifetime.'

'Yeah, I suppose so,' said Lucille. 'Let's have lunch.'

They flew across the garden in a great sweeping curve that they never could have done inside the dustbin. An old chicken was scratching about in the grass and round her feet five yellow chicks darted about like fluffy beetles. The chicken was picking up slugs and feeding them to her children, but as soon as she turned her back the children spat them out. The two bluebottles had never eaten slug before.

'It's quite nice,' said Attila, 'but not as good as fish heads.'

'They're probably too fresh,' said Lucille. 'If you kept them in rotten egg for a week or two, they'd probably taste better.'

After lunch they went and sat on the kitchen window sill. The sun had made the stone warm and the two flies felt quite drowsy.

'Do you suppose everything mum told us was untrue?' said Lucille.

'How do you mean?' asked Attila.

'You know. All that stuff about The Big Fish,' said Lucille.

'What, and the inside of the dustbin being the whole world?' said Attila.

'Yes.'

'Yes, I suppose it must have been,' said Attila. 'After all, when you think about it, it does all seem ridiculous.'

'You mean there's no Giant Flypaper and no Killer Aerosol?' said Lucille sarcastically.

'No, of course not,' said Attila. The two bluebottles laughed so much that all their eyes watered. Someone opened the window behind them and a thick sweet sugary smell drifted out. It rolled over them like a dream and made them feel quite giddy. They flew onto the window frame and look into the kitchen. In the middle of the table was a thick warm lemon meringue pie fresh from the oven.

'Isn't that wonderful?' said Lucille. 'Let's go and get some.'

'Hang on, hang on,' said Attila. 'What do you think we are – wasps? We're bluebottles. We eat rotten meat and dead fish.'

'But it smells so good,' said Lucille. 'Couldn't we just go and lick it a bit?'

'No, of course we can't,' said Attila, 'but I tell

133

you what we could do.'

'What, what?'

'We could go and be sick on it.'

So the two bluebottles flew into the house and buzzed round and round the kitchen table their heads all dizzy with the luscious smell of hot sugar. And there in the hot summer kitchen they discovered that not everything their mother had told them had been wrong. They had learnt that the world was a huge and wonderful place full of light and wide open skies. They had learnt that everywhere there were new and amazing things, that there was so much to see and to do, it seemed as if an endless life of adventure stretched out before them. And the very last thing they learnt as they swooped down towards the soft meringue mountains was that mother had certainly been right about one thing – The Massive Rolled Up Newspaper.

Arkwright the Cat

Winter came to the garden and plants that had stood tall and green all summer turned to gold and crumbled to dust. The skeletons of great thistles stood brown and lifeless, their dangerous spikes now no more than frail icicles crisp with frost. Between their shrivelled leaves the shells of insects turned to paper and blew away in the wind.

The swallows had gone to Africa, leaving their nests to sleeping spiders, while above them tortoiseshell butterflies hibernated in the roof. The birds that remained grew silent and lazy. They sat huddled in the bare branches fluffed up against the cold. With the flowers dead and gone the insects that had lived off them died too.

Below the old shed at the bottom of the garden the hedgehogs sank deep into their nest of grass and slept. The worms moved deeper into the earth to escape the cold and the moles tunnelled deeper to find them. At the bottom of the pond, next year's mosquitos and dragonflies lay suspended in tiny eggs and above the city the timeless stars flickered in the clear cold air of night.

Nature slowed down until it had almost stopped.

In the yard beside the house the wind picked up the loose leaves and threw them in a pile by the back door until it had made a golden pyramid against the step. It whistled round the corner and rattled past the dustbins as sharp as a rusty knife. Arkwright the cat sat in the coal bunker and listened as the wind roared round the house.

'Maybe it's just my memory playing tricks,' he thought to himself, 'but the wind seemed softer in the old days.'

'Maybe it's because I'm getting old,' he thought, 'and my fur is growing thin, but it didn't seem to be so cold either.'

He drifted off into dreams of long hot summer days when he and Gertrude had been the most feared creatures along the whole canal. No bird or mouse had been safe as they swept like tigers through the grass. Even tiny moths had flown away as they had approached.

The years had passed and they had grown old and slow. A year ago, Gertrude had crept into a tunnel under a mountain of old railway sleepers. Arkwright had sat by the dark hole and waited but he had known she wasn't coming out again.

A sparrow hopped down the yard but Arkwright was too cold to move. All he had eaten for the past few days had been the last moths of autumn that had flown into the street lights. There was nothing much else to eat in this quiet tidy street. It wasn't the sort of place where people threw scraps out. He'd found a few crusts thrown out for the birds but as soon as people saw him on their lawns they chased him away. He had grown so thin that every breath of cold reached into his bones.

He had grown up wild among the factories across the canal. There were dozens of cats there, dirty scraggy creatures that fought and screamed in the night.

He had had his day, when he had been top cat and all the others moved aside as he'd passed. It hadn't lasted long. It never did. After one proud summer when he was five years old, another younger cat had pushed him aside and over the next five years he had moved further and further away from the centre of things until he found himself with the old cats who scratched around in the younger ones' left overs. His companions then had been one-eared, half-blind, limping creatures hiding in dark corners. Arkwright hadn't been like the rest of them. He still had all his ears and teeth and, although slowed by age, he still walked straight and proud.

After Gertrude died, Arkwright felt restless and unwelcome. He sat by the canal and looked across the brown water at the tall trees and thick bushes alive with birds and butterflies, and said to himself, 'That's where I'll go, over there to that beautiful garden.' He walked along the canal in both directions for miles and miles but there was no way across. From time to time an old barge moved slowly along the water with its engine purring softly like a heartbeat. The warm smells of coal fires and cooking food drifted across the water as they passed. Ducks moved lazily aside and then the canal fell quiet again. If he had been younger he would have jumped onto one and waited until it had gone close to the opposite bank and leapt off, but he was too tired and stiff in his bones. So he just sat and watched them as they went by.

'How can I get across the water?' he asked the other cats.

'Too good to live here with the rest of us, are you?' they said and stopped speaking to him. Arkwright left the old lorry where most of the cats lived and moved into an oil drum by the towpath. And then one winter night there was a great storm and lightning struck a giant oak and it fell across the canal, crushing the lorry as it came. In the morning when the wind and rain had faded away there was a path over the water to the wonderful garden. The other cats had fled into the desert of factories, too scared to go near the wrecked lorry or the water.

'If we were meant to be on that side of the canal

we'd have been born there,' they said, but Arkwright saw his chance and scrambled through the tangled branches to the opposite bank. Later on, when some of the others had changed their minds, it was too late. Men had come and taken the tree away and the bridge to freedom had gone. On calm nights Arkwright could still hear the others across the water, fighting and squabbling.

He had been eleven years old when he had crossed the canal and now he was fifteen. He had had four good years, with plenty to eat and a warm dry home. In those years the house had been empty and Arkwright had lived in the cellar in an old rat's nest of warm newspapers. Away from the fighting and squabbling he had felt himself a king again. There were very few cats on this side of the water and those there were poor pampered creatures who avoided him. He had been lonely but he had felt at peace.

Then the people had moved into the house. They had closed up the hole into the cellar and Arkwright had spent the summer among the bushes and undergrowth. It had been a good summer, warm and well fed, but now winter had arrived and Arkwright began to feel his age. He was scared of people. He had seen the way they treated the cats around the factories and he knew man was something to keep away from, but the coal bunker was the only place he could find out of the biting wind.

143

At night he crept out into the garden to look for food. He had a terrible pain in his front leg that made him walk with a slow limp, so slow that any thought of catching mice was out of the question. Soft yellow light shone from the house onto the lawn carrying with it the warm smell of food and the sound of laughing voices. Next door's cat was inside its house, in the warmth by the fire and Arkwright found himself wondering if maybe all humans weren't the same.

'Maybe some of them are alright,' he thought, but when he tried to follow next door's cat into its kitchen a thin woman threw a jug of water over him. A frost fell that night and the water froze in his fur and Arkwright lay in the coal bunker wishing he could just go quietly to sleep and never wake up again. But he didn't, he just sat in the coal dust and shivered until morning.

The frost stayed all day now and the people in the house turned up their new central heating and decided to light the fire. The man brushed away the leaves from the coal bunker lid and opened it. At first he didn't see the two yellow eyes staring up out of the blackness. Only when Arkwright ran limping out of the shute at the bottom did the man realise the cat was there. He called him, but of course Arkwright stayed hidden in the bushes.

When the old cat crept back to his shelter that night, there was a saucer just inside the door, a saucer of white liquid that Arkwright had never seen before, but he knew what it was.

'Poison,' he muttered.

He had seen dishes of it in the factories and seen what had happened to the rats and cats that had eaten it. Later that night a hedgehog stuck its nose in and drank the liquid. Arkwright thought he should warn the poor animal but whenever he'd said anything in the past they'd all cursed him.

'Still,' he thought, 'I'm the only one who's lived past ten.' And then as the wind got colder he wondered if that had been such a great thing to achieve.

The next night the man put another saucer down and the hedgehog came back and emptied it.

'Was it you here last night?' asked Arkwright.

'What if it was?' asked the hedgehog.

'Do you feel alright?' said Arkwright.

'What're you talking about?' said the hedgehog.

'The poison,' said Arkwright.

'What poison?'

'The poison in the saucer,' said Arkwright.

'That's not poison,' laughed the hedgehog. 'That's milk.' As soon as he'd said it he realised what an idiot he'd been. If he'd let Arkwright keep on believing the saucer was full of poison, he'd be able to come and drink it every night. Now the cat would get it.

And the cat did get it. He sat in the bushes until the man had gone back indoors and then he hurried over and drank every last drop. After two weeks he no longer bothered to hide. The man spoke gently to him as he put down the saucer and Arkwright's ancient fear began to soften. The man's children began to come too and they brought food as well as milk. They held out their small hands to Arkwright but he wasn't ready to touch them. A lifetime of avoiding man, and avoiding him with good reason, couldn't just vanish and although instinct drew him towards the children other older instincts from untamed ancestors kept him back. He was not a cat who had once been loved by humans and abandoned to go wild. He had been born wild to parents who had been wild.

As November became December Arkwright grew stronger. With food and drink each day he became fatter and his fur thickened against the cold. The children put a box with a cushion in it inside the coal bunker but still he wouldn't let them go near him. Every day when they came to feed him, they held out their hands and talked to him. Every day he sat at a safe distance and listened to them. He was unable to undertand the words but he felt from the way they spoke that they meant him no harm.

'Come on cat,' said the boy, 'come and live in the house.'

'Come on pussie,' said the girl, 'please.'

But Arkwright kept them at ten arms' lengths.

Although he was growing fatter and warmer, the arthritis in his front leg got no better. In fact it was getting worse. Sometimes the effort of walking hurt so much that he could barely move. The pain seemed to spread through his whole body, even into the deepest corners of his brain. Only when he lay on his cushion and kept perfectly still did it get any better.

And that was how they caught him. The man came out with the saucer and as Arkwright tried to run away, the pain shot through him like a knife of fire and his leg collapsed beneath him. The man reached down and scooped him up and before he could spit or scratch he was in the house by the fire. For everyone, there are times when they have to stop struggling, times when they have to shrug their shoulders and let things happen. For Arkwright it was that time. He saw the dancing flames of the fire, felt its sunshine sinking into his cold fur and realised that he had been cold for too long. The flames flickered and swayed in front of his eyes and, like humans and animals everywhere, he was hypnotised.

With the warmth of the house and the pills they gave him, the pain in his leg grew less and less. For the rest of his life he walked with a limp, but as long as he could jump up onto the little girl's bed he didn't care that he couldn't stalk mice. He lay in the soft quilt at the child's feet and dreamt of Gertrude.

'If she could see me now,' he thought, 'what would she think?'

On Christmas day they gave Arkwright a collar. It was red velvet and had a medallion with his address on it.

'I'm not going anywhere,' he thought.

And he didn't, though when they started calling him Susie he did wonder about it.

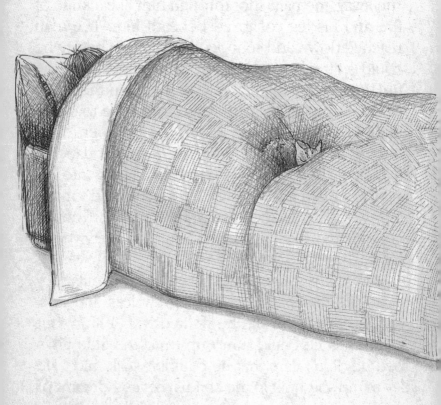